THE SECRET SCIENCE PROJECT THAT ALMOST ATE THE SCHOOL

by Judy Sierra

PICTURES by STEPHEN GAMMELL

A Paula Wiseman Book
Simon & Schuster Books for Young Readers
New York London Toronto Sydney

SIMON & SCHUSTER BOOKS FOR YOUNG READERS
An imprint of Simon & Schuster Children's Publishing Division
1230 Avenue of the Americas, New York, New York 10020

Book design by Einav Aviram
The text for this book is set in Malonia Voigo.
The illustrations for this book are rendered in watercolor, colored pencil, and pastel.
Manufactured in China
4 6 8 10 9 7 5
Library of Congress Cataloging-in-Publication Data
Sierra, Judy.
The secret science project that almost ate the school / Judy Sierra ; illustrated by Stephen Gammell.- 1st ed.
p. cm.
"A Paula Wiseman book."
Summary: A girl sends off for "Professor Swami's Super Slime" to use as her science fair project
and then has to cope with the funny disaster that follows.
ISBN-13: 978-1-4169-1175-3
ISBN-10: 1-4169-1175-8
[1. Science projects-Fiction. 2. Stories in rhyme.] I. Gammell, Stephen, ill. II. Title.
PZ8.3.S577Sec 2007
[E]-dc22
2005008421

To everyone at Grant Elementary School, San Lorenzo, California
—Judy

To Miss Fry and the second-grade class at Webster School in Des Moines, Iowa, 1951
—Stephen

I was grumpy, I was grouchy, I was slouching in my chair.
I was thinking grim and gloomy thoughts about the science fair.

Miranda bragged her rocket ship could travel to the moon.
Alexander taught his hamster how to sing a tune.
The ants on Mary's ant farm were growing corn and peas,
And Kevin Fink was on the brink of curing a disease.

Miss Fidget looked me in the eye. I wished that I could hide.
"What will **your** project be?" she asked.
"It's secret," I replied.

The secret was, I didn't really have a project yet.
I needed an experiment that no one would forget,
So I stayed up late and found a great one on the Internet.

A SCIENCE PROJECT FULLY GUARANTEED TO WIN FIRST PRIZE.

A SUBSTANCE SO AMAZING JUDGES WON'T BELIEVE THEIR EYES.

A MUTANT YEAST WITH JUST A PIECE OF DRAGON DNA.

PROFESSOR SWAMI'S

Super Slime

CO TOO
ARE YOU GOOEY?
FAMOUS BLOBS
HISTORY OF SLIME
STICKY STORIES
ABOUT PROFESSOR SWAMI

ORDER YOURS TODAY!

I sent the money instantly, then early Friday morning
A box appeared—it looked so weird—with big green letters:

WARNING!

YOUR SUPERSLIME IS SENSITIVE,
SO HANDLE IT WITH CARE.
KEEP IT SAFE INSIDE THIS BOX
UNTIL THE SCIENCE FAIR.

THEN FEED IT SUGAR TILL
IT SWELLS 1,000 TIMES IN MASS.
STAND BACK AS IT ERUPTS
INTO A HARMLESS CLOUD OF GAS.

I popped the lid and gave the slime a teeny-tiny poke.
It started getting bigger. It growled and blew off smoke.

It catapulted from the box and splattered on the floor

Precisely as Sir Scratchalot stepped through the kitty door

And plopped his paws in mutant muck—he rudely hissed and spat.

Yikes! The secret science project ate my kitty cat.

"Is that your stupid science project?" asked my sister Kate.

"Stop!" I said. "You'll hurt its feelings." **Oops!** It was too late.

The slime began to spin around. It rose into the air,

And when it roared, and hit the floor, my sister wasn't there.

Just then I heard my father's voice. "What's going on in there?

Something in that bedroom smells like moldy underwear."

"My science project's sensitive," I warned. "Don't make it mad."

There wasn't time to stop the crime. **The slime ingested Dad.**

The science project looked at **me.** I thought I saw it drool.

I tried to run away, but—**yikes!**—it followed me to school.

Miss Fidget shouted, "**Eeew! What is that big, disgusting creature?**"

The slime stopped short, and gave a snort,

and **ATE MY THIRD-GRADE TEACHER.**

It grew larger by the minute as it swallowed Alexander,

And incorporated Kevin Fink and Mary and Miranda.

As the slime was busy slurping up the last of Mary's ants,

I remembered the instructions in the pocket of my pants.

"Sugar!"

I commanded. **"Feed that hungry slime some sweets."**

Kids reached in their backpacks. Soon the air was filled with treats.

As doughnuts flew, and cookies, too, and candy bars and gum,

The bloated blob was quick to gobble every single crumb.

I shook a can of soda pop and sprayed the growing slime

Till I could tell that it had swelled at least a thousand times.

"Now everybody hide!" I screamed.

KA-FLAMM!

KA-
FLAZZ!

It vanished in a stupefying burst of CO_2.

KA-
FLOO!

When the dust had cleared away, my dad was up a tree.
My teacher dangled from the roof. We all were on TV.
"Sir Scratchalot!" I called and called. "What happened to my cat?"
"He's on your head," my sister said, "pretending he's a hat."

My project didn't win first prize, and that was fair . . . I guess. . . .
Miss Fidget kept me after school to clean up all the mess.
And underneath the cookie bits and sugary debris
I saw a goopy glob of slime and—yikes!—it winked at me!